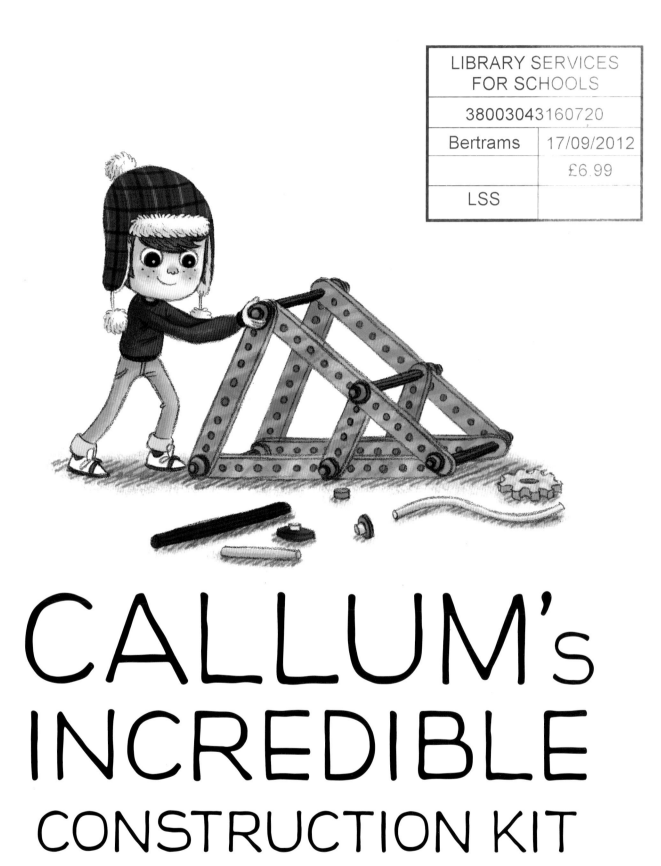

CALLUM's INCREDIBLE
CONSTRUCTION KIT

Jonathan Emmett   Illustrated by Ben Mantle

It was **Callum's** birthday and he'd almost finished opening his presents.

"One last surprise," said Dad, "but it's in the garage."

The garage was full of boxes.

"What is it?" asked Mum.

"It's a CONSTRUCTION KIT!" gasped Callum.

"It's an old one," said Dad. "They don't make them like this any more."

"I LOVE IT!" said Callum.

Callum played with the kit **every** day.

He started off ...

building small things ...

that didn't
always work!

But as he went on

1

16 x
32 x
30 x
17 x
2 x
2 x
18 x
18 x
2 x
1 x
1 x
3 x
1 x
1 x

2

he built BIGGER...

3

and BIGGER...

...and BIGGER!

Callum took the kit **everywhere** he went…

even on **holiday!**

"I never know
when I might need it,"
Callum explained.

"And you have
to admit …

it can be

Mum thought that Callum already
had enough pieces, but Callum
was always looking for more.

And before long, he had so much kit ...

...it filled every room in the house!

"What's that groaning noise?" asked Callum, as the family sat down for dinner.

Before anyone could answer, a chunk of ceiling fell onto the table and large cracks began appearing in the walls!

Everyone scrambled outside as ...

...the whole house came crashing to the ground!

"It must have been the weight of Callum's kit," said Dad.

Callum was pulling pieces of kit
out of the rubble.

"It's all right," he grinned.
"None of it seems to be broken!"

Mum and Dad looked at Callum
in amazement.

"Never mind the kit. What about
OUR HOUSE?!"
shouted Mum.

But Callum was still smiling.

"Don't worry about that,"
he said.

ANOTHER ONE!"

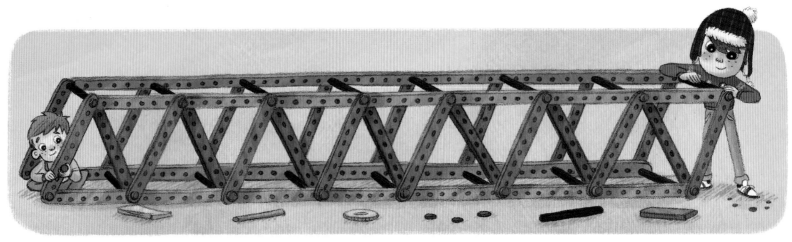

"We can always…

...BUILD

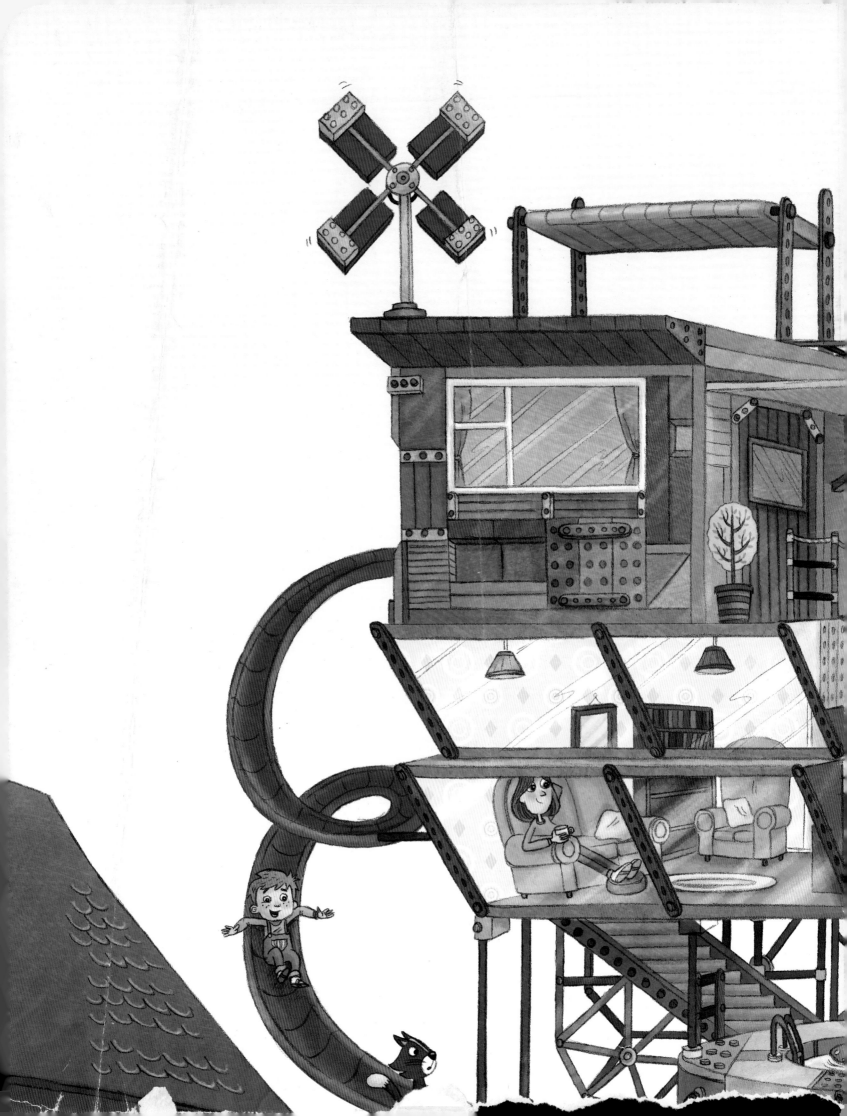

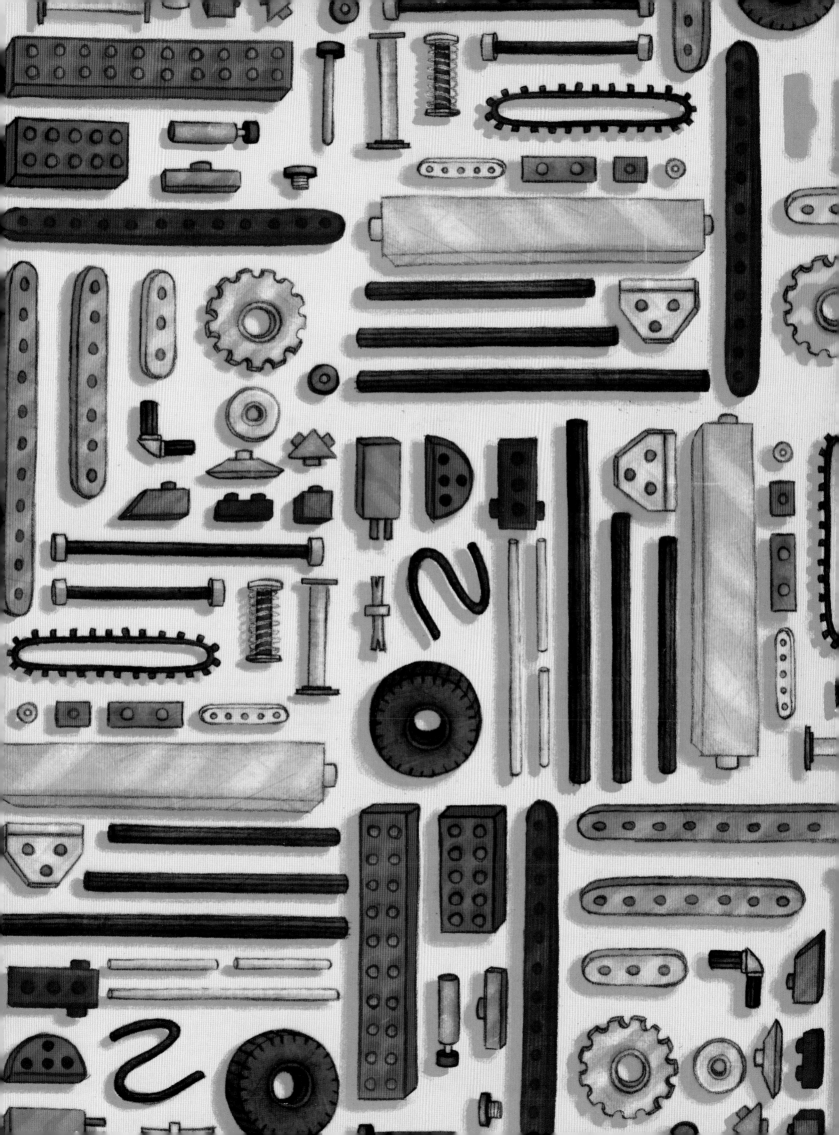